INVISIBLE

PUFFIN BOOKS

UK | USA | Canada | Ireland | Australia
India | New Zealand | South Africa

Puffin Books is part of the Penguin Random House group of companies
whose addresses can be found at global.penguinrandomhouse.com.

www.penguin.co.uk
www.puffin.co.uk
www.ladybird.co.uk

First published in the USA by Balzer + Bray, an imprint of HarperCollins Publishers, 2017
Published in Great Britain by Puffin Books 2017

001

Copyright © Terri Libenson, 2017

The moral right of the author/illustrator has been asserted

Printed in Italy by L.E.G.O. S.p.A

A CIP catalogue record for this book is available from the British Library

ISBN: 978-0-141-37223-5

All correspondence to:
Puffin Books
Penguin Random House Children's
80 Strand, London WC2R 0RL

www.greenpenguin.co.uk

MIX
Paper from
responsible sources
FSC
www.fsc.org
FSC® C018179

Penguin Random House is committed to a
sustainable future for our business, our readers
and our planet. This book is made from Forest
Stewardship Council® certified paper.

For Mike, Mollie, and Nikki
(and thirteen-year-old Terri, who inspired this book)

bangs explosion

pre-braces

my mom still dressed me

PRELOGUE (Yes, that's a thing.)

This is me.

You're probably wondering how I became a puddle of slime.

Easily explained. It happened in a day. Okay, five hours, if you want to get technical. It also involved a really embarrassing incident. I'll get to that.

I never thought I was much to look at to begin with, but a puddle of slime **really** isn't very attractive. I'm hoping to return to human form soon.

puddle of slime
even less attractive
with hair and
eyeballs

In the meantime let me start from the beginning. Or, in this case, the . . .

PROLOGUE

There are a whole lot of books about kids who are outcasts. I've probably read them all.

Usually, the story goes something like this:

(1) The main character is weird . . .

crazy eyes →

smart . . .

glasses to prove smartitude →

← beanie to prove nerdity

or has some kind of disability.

(2) The character gets picked on.

(3) The character gets revenge . . .

or turns the situation around so that "lessons are learned."

(4) Along the way, the character picks up one or two equally geeky friends so he or she isn't alone.

It's all good, but what about books starring other kinds of kids? You know, the ones who aren't exactly weird . . .

or smart . . .

or . . . well, this.

The ones who are maybe . . . heroes-in-waiting.

And what if this "hero" isn't picked on?

What if the hero just goes . . . unnoticed?

EMMIE

My name is Emmie Douglass. I'm thirteen and in seventh grade.

shortish
curly hair
that sticks
out

school (also
kind of flat)

LAKEFRONT

flat as a
pancake

twig
legs

super stretchy backpack
[contents: binders, sketchbook,
Sharpie, 32½ colored pencils,
pencil sharpener, lunch, key,
broken hair tie, squashed lip balm]

I was born here in Lakefront. My parents say I came into the world with a "howl that rattled the windows." They say it like it's the funniest thing in the world.

"Irony," my dad calls it.

I call it "false expectations."

then

now

a tie for muteness

So yeah, if you haven't guessed, I'm pretty quiet. Been this way since I can remember. That newborn thing must've been a fluke. But then, I have much older, louder siblings. My mom says I was chattier when I was little, so my theories are:

(a) I got tired of trying to be heard over my sibs and clammed up, or . . .

(b) once they got older and busier, I didn't have anyone to talk to except grown-ups. And who wants to talk to grown-ups?

By the way, having siblings so much older than me makes me something called an "oops baby." I try not to think about that.

EWWW!

the one and only time I thought about it

Anyway, now Brandon and Trina are in college and out of the house. My parents work, so I'm by myself even more.

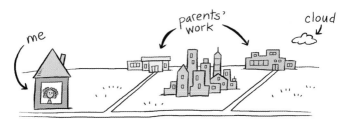

It wasn't always like this. When my brother and sister were young, my mom stayed home to raise them. They always had friends over, and the house got pretty loud. I think by the time I came along, my parents were ready for a permanent getaway. That meant my mom getting a new job at the fitness center and my dad putting in fifty hours a week as an IT manager (whatever that is). Anyway, now the house is pretty quiet.

Before you start feeling sorry for me, let me set things straight. My parents don't neglect me. They're just busy people. When we're together, they pay attention to me. They even make eye contact and stuff.

I guess because I'm the last kid left in the house, my parents want some time away. Still, when they are home, they kind of hover.

Sometimes I think I need something in between.

My mom is a health nut and decided to turn that into her "second act." That's why she has the fitness center job. She's a part-time receptionist and part-time cardio instructor. She has more muscles in her big toe than I do in my entire body.

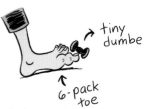

tiny dumbe

6-pack toe

Along with fitness, she makes meals with things like "quinoa" and "wheat berries" ... not to mention the latest fruit or vegetable of the month.

bowl o' steamed tofu and kale-arugula hybrid

Let's just say our bathroom gets a workout, too.

≈flush≈

My dad and I are more alike. We're both quiet, but he's better with math and numbers. We can sit together for hours without talking. You'd think that would be awkward.

Okay, it is.

But it can also be nice.

As far as friends go, I do have a best one. Her name's Brianna. We've been friends since she moved here from Atlanta when we were in kindergarten. Brianna lives exactly nine minutes away by car and about a hundred minutes away by walking (or twenty-eight minutes away by bike, if you want to get really technical). More on Bri later.

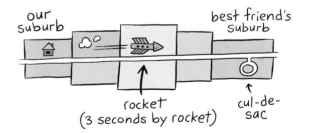

our suburb

best friend's suburb

rocket
(3 seconds by rocket)

cul-de-sac

When I'm by myself, my favorite thing to do is draw. I like it better than watching TV. Probably because there's nothing on that I'm really interested in.

I'm also really good at it. I'm not great at other things (like sports), but art makes me feel like there's something I can do that not a lot of others can.

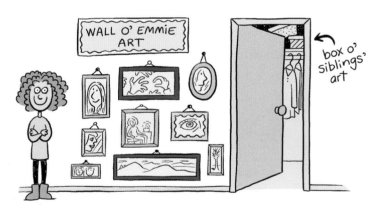

Anyway, I'm pretty bad at the usual things that get people's attention:

That's pretty much my background in a nutshell. It isn't very interesting. But I like to think that someday it will be.

It just **has** to be.

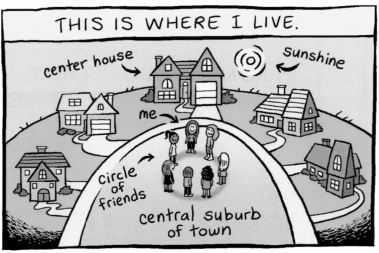

I HAVE LOTS OF HOBBIES. I LIKE FASHION, MUSIC, AND ORGANIZING SMALL SOCIAL EVENTS.

Katie, I don't think all your friends will fit in the house.

I ALSO PLAY SPORTS, LIKE VOLLEYBALL. MY FRIENDS SAY I'M GOOD, BUT SOMETIMES THEY EXAGGERATE.

Woo! Katie!

you scored the winning point!

THWUNK

ON WEEKENDS, MY FRIENDS AND I HAVE SLEEPOVERS. FOR SOME REASON, THEY PREFER MY HOUSE.

More chocolate, fudge, taffy, and peanut butter cups, girls?

Yes, please!

URP

SOMETIMES WE GO TO THE MALL AND I MEET NEW PEOPLE.

Hi, I'm a Hollywood scout looking for an all-American girl to star in the next **Big Teen Movie.** Interested?

'kay.

CONTRACT

SOME CALL ME LUCKY,
BUT I WORK HARD FOR
EVERYTHING I HAVE.

I practice volleyball on weekends. →

THWUN-KUH

I study every night.

← books I've memorized

I take good care of my skin. →

face lotion I patented

I call and text my BFFs to maintain friendships.

(14th BFF) → blah yah blah

BASICALLY, I'M JUST YOUR AVERAGE TEEN GIRL.

You've been crowned Homecoming Queen!

But I'm in middle school.

They made an exception for you.

(OKAY... MAYBE I'M A LITTLE LUCKY.)

EMMIE

Today is Monday, and I have to go to school. I really, **really** don't want to.

Even though I'm by myself a lot, it's better than school. School means: teachers, students, and things that died on the floor.

expired rodent in front of my locker

On weekdays I try to sleep in as long as I can. There's not much I can do with my spiral-y hair, and I'm not allowed to wear makeup yet, so I'm pretty much get-up-and-go.

or... get up and hit snooze 5 times

↓

#PUNCH

Breakfast time is pretty routine. I eat cereal, my dad cracks jokes to get me in a good mood, and my mom rushes around doing last-minute things.

5 minutes! Your hair set a new deflating record.

har

Where's my purse?

purse

Where are my keys?

keys

Where's my car?

in garage

As you can see, "routine" doesn't mean "calm."

Sometimes I miss my brother and sister. Even when they were arguing in the morning, they took most of the attention away from me. But that was a while ago. In fact, it's been over two years since they've been around.

← old photo

Once in a while I'll call Brandon or Trina in the morning, before their classes. I pretend I'm calling with an elaborate homework question (which is why I don't text), but really, I just miss their voices. They're surprisingly nicer, too, when they don't live here.

Today I don't have time to call them. Instead, I suck down my cereal while ignoring my dad's corny jokes and my mom's fussing. Soon enough, it's time to go.

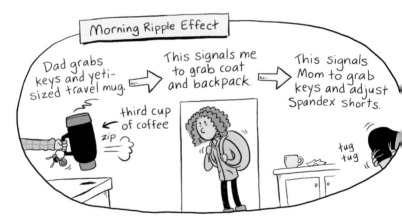

The good news is, I live close to the middle school, so I don't have to take the bus, which is the worst. I rode the bus in elementary school, and I'm still trying to block it out.

My dad drops me off on his way to work.
It's slightly better.

Whenever I walk into school, I start feeling **the knots**. That's when my stomach gets all tight, and I have to take exactly ten deep breaths to unsqueeze everything. I came up with this technique a few days after I started middle school. It helps keep me "centered," as my mom's DVD yoga lady says (my mom always brings home free DVDs from the fitness center). Yoga Lady's the one who inspired this exercise, but that's where it stops. She also says stuff like "flower your kidneys" and "Pluto has been disabled."

The first thing I do is go to my locker. The hallway is super-crowded, so I have to duck and weave to get there. I take great pains not to get bumped. That kind of body contact in middle school is frowned upon.

Down the hall, I see two boys having a conversation in front of my locker. Actually, it's less of a conversation and more of a primal-monkey noisefest.

Boys.

Great.

I can't talk to boys.

(Okay, I can't talk to anyone . . . but especially not to boys.)

I slow my pace, praying they'll see me and move in the next thirty seconds.

To stall, I pretend to text Brianna on my dumb phone. (One of those old-fashioned flip phones they used, like, ten or thirty years ago. It was my mom's. All I can do with it is make calls and send simple texts. My parents won't let me buy a smartphone until I'm in high school—which is so annoying because I have enough money in my bank account from birthdays to get one.)

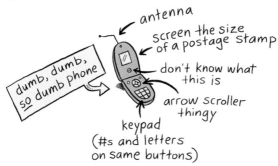

I don't actually text Brianna. She's probably busy doing early morning extra credit or curing cancer or something (more on her later). I just need time for those boys to see me.

Yeah, it doesn't work.
So I gather all my courage to speak.

I know they barely budged, but this is actually a minor victory. Usually, when I say something, people tend to get annoyed and ask me to repeat myself or speak up.

I find **that** somewhat annoying.

I take stock of my victory, put away my coat and backpack, grab my books, and stand there for a second. Locker #322 provides nice, private shelter . . . especially if you rest your head on the top shelf.

Sometimes I wonder . . . does anyone ever see me?
Do I even want them to?

29

THE HALL IS SUPERCROWDED, BUT EVERYBODY IS NICE ENOUGH TO STEP ASIDE.

m'lady

blushing

Thanks!

LIKE MY HOUSE, MY LOCKER IS IN THE CENTER OF EVERYTHING.

lockers of all the cute boys

Hurry, Katieee!

I HAVE A FEW MINUTES, SO I MAKE CONVO WITH MY GIRLS. WE DISCUSS MOVIES, VOLLEY-BALL, AND MY MATH STRUGGLES.

I'm pushing an A-.

Maybe Mr. Dodd can give you extra credit.

Wish I had an A-.

SOON A FEW FRIENDS JOIN US.
WE TALK ABOUT WINTER BREAK.

EVERYONE STARTS TALKING TO ME
AT ONCE (WHICH HAPPENS ALL THE
TIME). I DON'T WANT TO CAUSE
JEALOUSY AMONGST AMIGAS,
SO I INTERJECT.

EMMIE

Right before registration I meet up with Brianna. It's the only period I have with her besides lunch. She's in all the **advanced** classes.

We walk and talk. This is my favorite time of the day. I actually feel . . . normal.

When we get to registration we split up. Bri (last name: Davis) is seated on the left side of the room with the **Das–Des** while I'm seated on the right with the **Dos–Dus**. It's so unfair. I'm only a couple letters away from being her neighbor.

I sit down at my desk and keep to myself. Easy enough since most of us don't really know one another (or don't want to) really well. We're just grouped together because our names are close in the alphabet. I've been sitting behind Lindsay Donsky since sixth grade, and I think we've spoken exactly six words to each other.

Also, she's been dousing herself in cinnamon-ginger body spray all year and smells like eternal Christmas, so I've been too busy sneezing to say much (see above memory balloon).

Registration is where I get most of my homework done . . . a fact I keep from my parents. Easy enough. They got tired of helping my brother and sister with homework all those years ago, so by the time it was my turn, they encouraged me to be "an independent thinker." Therefore, I independently think I will do one-third of my homework at night and finish two-thirds in registration. This works about three-quarters of the time, as long as my dad isn't running late.

Anyway, here I sit, sandwiched between Lindsay Donsky and Kyle Duncan. Two popular people who talk over me as if I'm not there.

I start working on English, mainly to avoid math, my worst subject. I wish Bri sat next to me so she could help me.

As if she read my mind, I get a text from her. Glad I remembered to put my phone on vibrate. We're not supposed to have phones in class, but everyone does anyway. Once in a while teachers allow them for in-class assignments. Well, not **my** phone because it's, like, three thousand years old.

Anyway, I notice Bri's text and sneak a peek behind my English binder:

U going 2
talk 2 him
2day?

I respond (sarcastically).

yeah
rt.

clicky

The "he" she's referring to is . . .

Well, I'll get to that later.

Since we're still on the subject of my BFF, maybe now's a good time to tell you more about Brianna. Besides her big brain, I mean.

We've known each other since midkindergarten. I say "mid" because her family moved from Atlanta in December of that year. Her dad took a new job, and Bri has been mad at him each and every winter since.

still has "thin" Georgia skin

I think we became friends because I was always nice, and she was always kinda bossy.

It was a good match.

Put Ms. Wiggles in the high chair.

Okee.

Clean up "Connect Four"

Okay.

Jump up and down and bark like a puppy.

YAP YAP YAP

I told you Brianna is smart. That's not really a good description. "Gifted" is what teachers and parents say. She was always the smartest student in our elementary class. She aced the spelling bees and won all the science and math fair awards.

Even though she is supersmart, she is fun to hang out with (aside from her bossiness). We like the same music, movies, and books. We both have wild imaginations and make up a lot of pretend games. She even likes helping me with math, which I'm hopeless at.

out into the ether

Bri's parents got divorced right before fifth grade. I hate to admit, it was a tough time for her but a great time for me. She ended up having lots of sleepovers at my house.

Greetings from CAMP ROBO! xoxo

By the end of that year, Bri was happier, and we were totally inseparable. Well, except for the time she went to robotics camp for two weeks. Otherwise, we were always together.

But things changed when we got to middle school. We're still best friends, but she was put right into the gifted program, which left me alone. This was especially rough because Brianna managed to make new friends in her classes.

discussing quantum physics or Brainiatrics 101 or something

Remember her?

And the more alone I was, the quieter I got.

mouth literally disappeared

As I said, we're still best friends, though. And despite my shyness and everything, she gets me. She's about the only one who does. We have a lot of history.

a zillion chapters

Em and Bri's BIG BOOK of History!

Anyway, back to registration. Bri texts:

I'm gonna have 2 push u into his arms!!
:-P

I giggle, sigh, and get on with my homework. Or try to.

incoming

For the rest of the period, I take peeks at the other kids sneaking texts and notes back and forth or whispering over messy desks. They don't seem to mind if they're sitting next to friends or not. Anyone will do.

My stomach knots up a little.

Right before the bell rings, I realize I still have one more essay question to get through. I hurriedly scribble out a paragraph, vowing for the zillionth time to stop procrastinating (drawing) at night and finish all my homework at home.

scritchy
scritchy
scritch

Home.

Only seven hours and counting . . .

SINCE I GOT ALL MY HOMEWORK DONE AFTER VOLLEYBALL, I CAN CATCH UP ON IMPORTANT NEWS... LIKE THE GOING RUMOR:

So a certain 7th-grade *someone* likes you.

achoo!

squeal!

Back to your seat, miss Hilliard.

STILL, I TRY NOT TO LISTEN TO GOSSIP (EVEN IF IT'S FACTUALLY BASED).

How do you know?

A friend of a friend of his sister said so.

Aren't you excited, Katie?

yeah. He's the nicest, friendliest (cutest) boy in our grade.

I REALLY _AM_ EXCITED, BUT A RUMOR'S JUST A RUMOR.

It is true. I got it from the source's source's sister.

Uh... I think.

I TRY NOT TO GET TOO DISTRACTED WITH THOUGHTS OF _YOU-KNOW-WHO._ I PEOPLE-WATCH INSTEAD. I _LOVE_ PEOPLE-WATCHING.

Wow, everyone sure has a lot of homework.

Oh dang! I forgot to study for French.

Argh! Math.

SOMETIMES I FEEL LUCKY I'M SO ORGANIZED. YEP, LOTS OF TIME TO RELAX.

text text text

scritch scritch scritch

44

EMMIE

Off to first period. Brianna and I separate.

I make my way down the hallway/labyrinth, keeping to myself. My parents always tell me to lift my head and "walk tall."

That makes me wonder if they ever went to middle school. If they did, they'd understand that it's sometimes dangerous to lift your head. Something gross could fly at it.

I have to make a detour to use the girls' restroom. There's a line out the door.

20 girls at mirror putting on forbidden makeup ➔

flush

For a minute I think about skipping it, but I don't think I can make it through the next period. Also, my science teacher, Mr. Danker, is known for being stingy with the restroom passes. We learned that the first few days of class.

blah blah matter blah compound...

I wait forever.

And ever.

And ever. At this point, my bladder is in distress. ("Over-quenched," Yoga Lady would say.)

I start daydreaming to take my mind off pressing matters. I think about summer and wish it was June. Or winter break already. Or any time I don't have to be with crowds of people my age.

I think about a family trip we took to Niagara Falls when I was six and my siblings were still living at home. That was when I still talked. A lot. In fact, my brother had taken out his phone and recorded me going on for about forty-five minutes during the car ride. I talked nonstop about a playdate with Brianna. My family jokingly says they keep the recording for "evidence."

...an' then we chased her doggie, Loaf, awound a twee, an' then we ate ice cweam, an' then...

HA HA ha ha

yikes

It's really not **that** funny.

And anyway, thinking about Niagara Falls isn't helping my current situation.

Instead, I start thinking about another trip my parents and I took. It was to Chicago last spring. It was the one and only time they both decided to take a vacation from work. I remember standing in front of the huge bean sculpture at Millennium Park and making faces. And going to the art museum and seeing a bunch of paintings by Paul Klee (my favorite artist). And eating the best pizza of my life (although my dad, who's from New York, would totally disagree).

What I remember the most, though, is that the days seemed to be all about me—not in an annoying, embarrassing way . . . but in a cool, low-key kind of way. Everything was so relaxed. My parents were relaxed (not distracted or hammering me with questions). **I** was relaxed. And I got to choose where to go and what to do. **So** unlike middle school.

My daydream is interrupted by a loud flush. A stall finally empties. But then a huge girl behind me cuts in front.

Now I'm really late. When I get out, the halls are practically empty. This means I could get a tardy slip. That's bad.

Also, everyone will look at me when I walk into class. That's worse.

I rush to science and see everyone already sitting in their seats. Luckily, they're talking and not paying attention to me.

The teacher isn't here yet. I sit down quietly and wish for the hundredth time I had a seat at the back. I also wish I had someone to talk to. Like Bri.

jabber jabber

The gossip girls are on a roll today. I didn't think anyone could talk so much about nothing. I don't know whether to be weirded out or awed. Maybe both. You'd think after a while their jaws would start aching.

sling-like things for sore jabber jaws

Everybody has someone to talk to except me. I start getting that squeezy feeling in my stomach again. I take my ten breaths, but it's not working this time. Maybe my spine is unjuiced.

I go to Plan B. Inching my face as close to my homework notebook as possible, I start doodling.

I wait. And draw.

The more I draw, the more my stomach unknots.

I wish I could draw all day.

BEFORE FIRST PERIOD, I DO WHAT MOST GIRLS DO: MAKE A BEELINE FOR THE RESTROOM.

SEEMS THAT LUCK IS ON MY SIDE, 'CAUSE I MANAGE TO SNAG A GOOD SPOT IN LINE.

WOW. ZERO MIRROR SPACE TODAY. MORGAN MAKES ROOM NEAR THE WINDOWS, BUT NATURE CALLS.

THE HALLS ARE DEAD WHEN I STEP OUT.

HOPE I DON'T GET A TARDY SLIP. IT'S HARD TO TALK YOUR WAY OUT OF ONE.

WHEN I GET TO CLASS, THE TEACHER IS NOWHERE IN SIGHT (YAY!).

THERE'S THAT QUIET GIRL. SHE LIKES TO DRAW. I'D RATHER TALK. OR TEXT.

NOW, I'M A NICE PERSON, BUT I'M NOT A PUSHOVER. HEARING MY NAME COME OUT OF JOE'S MOUTH, I GIVE HIM A WITHERING GLARE. HE COWERS.

Sorry I'm late. Let's get started.

withering stare that can go above heads

Whatever. Here.

POOR GIRL. BUT HONESTLY, I DON'T UNDERSTAND PEOPLE WHO DON'T STICK UP FOR THEMSELVES.

IT'S NOT LIKE IT TAKES EFFORT.

EMMIE

Usually, I don't like being the last person out of the classroom, but today I take my time. I have gym next.

pretending to be
absorbed in boo
stacking and
paper shufflin

I believe PE was invented to torture students, like all those other things teachers used to get away with back in the days when my parents went to school.

paddling backsides
on birthdays

WHACK

Censored

Teach-
ers'
Lounge

COUGH
HACK

secondhand smoke

When you're trying to play it cool, gym class is not the place to be. 'Cause eventually, you have to TAKE A TURN at something.

Nothing ever goes right in gym. I mean nothing. Unless you're one of those sporty, coordinated types.

Sometimes I wish I got my mom's athletic genes. Then again, she didn't get into fitness until after she had me. But suddenly—**BOOM**—she started doing 5Ks, then 10Ks, then half marathons, then extreme cardio classes and SoulCycling and power yoga and . . . Well, let's just say her "second act" receives lots of standing ovations.

My mom says she started out like me and never did anything athletic. She calls me a "late bloomer" and says it will probably kick in when I'm older. At the rate I'm going, that might not be for a while.

↖ me at 90

Today we have fitness skills. That's gotta be the worst kind of class ever invented (aside from math). To Coach Durdle's credit, she shows us how to do everything first, and we get a lot of practice.

To her discredit, she uses students to demonstrate each skill (and we get a lot of practice).

Of course, today she picks Quiet Girl to demonstrate the first skill: straight-legged toe touches.

But believe it or not, even gym isn't the worst part of gym.

The worst part is the locker room. You have to get changed in front of everyone.

And then get changed back **again**.

I don't know why I feel so self-conscious. It's not like anyone is looking at me.

I guess being quiet, skinny, and flat sometimes has its advantages.

WHEN THE BELL RINGS FOR GYM, I RACE TO THE LOCKER ROOM.

A LOT OF MY FRIENDS ARE IN GYM. THEN AGAIN, A LOT OF FRIENDS ARE IN ALL MY CLASSES. GUESS I'M LUCKY.

TODAY WE'RE DOING FITNESS SKILLS. COACH DURDLE ASKS ME TO DEMONSTRATE PROPER CRUNCHES.

See, class? Katie holds her neck straight.

abs of steel

abs of steel-cut oatmeal

I MESS UP ONCE OR TWICE. SOMETIMES IT'S HARD BEING IN THE SPOTLIGHT.

oops (giggle)

girl, you crazy!

AFTER FITNESS SKILLS, WE'RE LEFT TO DO WHAT WE WANT. THAT USUALLY MEANS LOUNGING ON THE GYMNASTICS EQUIPMENT AND GABBING.

yadda yabba boys gabba science test blah blah more boys

BONK

EMMIE

I've got English next. For once I'm not late leaving gym, so I take my time walking to class. I hate being the last one in, but being the first is almost as bad.

(the goal: English)

bad posture (parents would have a fit)

semifunctional water fountain to linger at

← meandering feet

gossip girls

Tyler Ross (dreamy)

Anthony Rand (6th cutest boy in class, but sp

After pausing at the water fountain, I pass my crush, Tyler Ross. He doesn't look at me. Then again I'm only looking at his stomach.

Well, at least he finally noticed me.

I should probably backtrack and tell you about Tyler Ross. We went to elementary school together.

not as flat

LAKEFRONT ELEMENTARY

lake about 10 miles away ⇨

He didn't know I existed then, and he doesn't now. That's too bad 'cause I reached my cuteness peak when we met.

Tyler Ross (cute as two buttons)

me (cute as a button)

← Brianna

That was in kindergarten. But my crush started when I dropped my favorite Hello Kitty eraser on the hallway floor in fourth grade, and he picked it up. He gave it back to me and

D.A.R.E.

Student of the month →

smiled. Or half smiled. I don't even know if he really saw me. But that was enough. I fell hard.

I even remember going home that afternoon and trying to re-create his face on paper.

At first I didn't tell anyone about my crush, not even Brianna. I think part of me wanted to keep it a secret because if I admitted it out loud, I would jinx it.

Eventually, in fifth grade, I got tired of keeping it a secret and told her. It was a huge relief. Bri confessed that she liked Anthony Randall (spitty boy). Don't ask me why.

Tyler Ross and Anthony Randall were best friends, just like us, and they always hung out together. That made it easy for Bri and me to ~~stalk~~ follow them around. We'd wait until they walked home from school, and we'd stay about half a block behind them so they wouldn't see us. We were lucky we were never caught.

Eventually, my mom found out about my crush. She acciden-tally overheard me talking to Bri during a sleepover. At least, I **think** it was an accident.

I made her swear not to tell Dad.

Then I made her swear to never bring it up again.

Over the years I learned a lot about Tyler Ross. For instance, he's good at sports and has a lot of friends. He gets good grades (As and Bs). He plays the trumpet in band. He wears a lot of orange. He has a raised freckle under his right eye. I only know that because he once collected our math tests, and I didn't realize it was him until I looked up. For some reason the freckle jumped out at me.

But what I really, really like about him is his smile. He smiles a lot (even with braces!). And he's friendly and nice. Well, except when goofball girls are tripping in front of him.

← dreamy and shiny

And in the last year or so, I've finally mastered capturing his likeness on paper.

TR + ED

Tyler Ross

me

Anyway, back to English. It's the only class where I sit at the back. If we're not writing, I draw. Mrs. Winn is pretty clueless and never notices.

actually closes her eyes when she speaks

at
on
in

Truth is, I'm pretty good at this class. (I have an A-.) I think it's because when I draw, I can actually focus better. Is that weird?

stuff actually sticking to my brain

I also like this class because Tyler Ross sits two seats diagonally in front of me and I can stare at the right side of his back. Today he's wearing an orange-and-gray shirt with a small fuzzball on it.

imagining picking at the fuzzball, just to touch his shoulder

It would be so great to touch his shoulder. Or talk to him.

scritch

Sometimes I wonder if he notices me at all.

TYLERASKEDMEOUTTYLERASKED MEOUTTYLERASKEDMEOUT!!!!!

EMMIE

Lunch. Brianna and I have regular seats in the caf. They're in the back, near the ice cream freezer. We sit at the same table as Sophia Gresker, Lizzie Freed, and a few other kids from art club. Except there are about three empty seats between us and them.

art club kids →

token Emo girl ↓

me ↓   Brianna ↓

Every two minu[tes] someone slam[s] the lid, which shakes the table.

Bri and I both eat packed lunches. Bri, because she's a picky eater. It's not that she has allergies or anything. She just eats only, like, three or four foods: plain pizza, sausage pizza, and Hawaiian pizza. Oh yeah, and vanilla yogurt—covered peanuts, which is weirdly specific. I want to tell her that she's not six years old and she should try other things, but Bri would probably just scoff and make a face at my eggplant-quinoa salad. I can't really blame her for that.

eggplant bits

quinoa (pronounced KEEN-wah)

not as bad as it looks (or smells)

spork

As for me, well . . . it's my mom. She doesn't really control what or how much I eat . . . but she does control what comes in the house. That means:

CHIPS

COOKIES

processed meats

processed anything (??)

sodium benzoate

not sure what this is

At least I'm allowed to buy lunch once a week. But I have to use my allowance. And since I just spent it on a new sketch pad,

I'm eating last night's eggplant-quinoa salad.

so organic it moved

The cafeteria is jam-packed because both seventh and eighth graders use it. You'd think the loud, crowded, clique-y caf would give me major stress issues, but since Brianna is with me, I don't mind it much. Except when she's at home sick or something. That's when I hide out in the library.

Today our little corner is louder than usual. All the students of the month earned free ice cream sandwiches, so the freezer lid-slamming is at a record high.

Partly to distract ourselves and partly for fun, Brianna suggests we write really gushy, sappy love notes to our crushes. Not that we would give the notes to them or anything.

We make up games like this a lot. We've done stuff like mixing a bunch of disgusting cafeteria ingredients and then challenging each other to eat it without gagging (the worst was pizza cheese/mayonnaise/fro-yo). Or my favorite game: spork sculpting.

Speaking of sporks, we once challenged each other to invent other utensils that do two things at once. We came up with twenty-four.

some favorites

whiskula   knorf   straidle

Today I agree to go along with the love note game.
We think for a few minutes and jot down some thoughts.

The cornier the better!

We can try to outdo each other.

HA HA

10 minutes later

Ready?

Oh man. (giggle) Almost.

She reads a few more silly stanzas. I'm giggling wildly.

Apparently, mine is more honest-gushy than funny-gushy.

The bell suddenly rings. I grab our notes and shove them into my English binder. I have health next, but I've gotta stop at my locker first, so I rush out.

art kids and their luggage

LUNCH. MY FRIENDS AND I HAVE A SWEET SEAT IN THE CAF, RIGHT IN THE MIDDLE OF EVERYTHING. THERE ARE SO MANY OF US, WE'RE ALLOWED TO MOVE TWO TABLES TOGETHER.

TYLER IS STARING AT ME, BUT I PRETEND NOT TO PAY ATTENTION. MORGAN SAYS IT KEEPS THE BOYS INTERESTED.

pretending to be in deep conversation, but really talking about YouTube videos

I USUALLY DON'T LIKE BEING WATCHED, BUT WHEN TYLER DOES IT, I FEEL DIFFERENT. LIKE, *ADORED*.

STILL, I TRY TO PLAY IT COOL ALL THROUGH LUNCH.

WHEN THE BELL RINGS, I RUSH OUT AND STOP AT MY LOCKER. I GRAB MY BOOKS AND FRESHEN MY LIP GLOSS.

EMMIE

By this time of day my stomach knots have usually subsided. Sure, it takes about four hours for that to happen, but a victory is a victory.

So when I walk to my locker to exchange my books and put away my lunch bag, I walk a little taller. Of course, I'm putting my head at risk, but my mom and Yoga Lady would be proud of my "blooming spine."

prelunch stomach

very squeezy

postlunch stomach

whew

almost normalish

vertebrae less scrunchy

head more vertical

smelly kid more smelly from gym

As soon as I get to health class, Mr. Bauman announces that the heat has gone out in the room and we have to relocate to the library while it's being fixed. Says we'll have free time until we get back.

This is good news. I love the library. It's superquiet and peaceful. My kind of environment. Plus, the librarian loves me.

We walk to the library as a class. Aaand ... double good news!

This is so cool. Bonus Bri time! We huddle together at a table.

We settle on an agreement: Brianna will study and I will sketch her. Maybe I'll absorb some of her information if I concentrate hard enough.

Bri isn't always the most patient person, but she'll let me draw her while she studies or does homework. Probably 'cause she's so focused, she barely notices anything else.

(Some things don't change.)

When I sketch for a long time, something happens: my mind starts to drift off. It's like when people say they're driving and they totally check out and can't remember how they got from Point A to Point B.

That's how it is with me. My hand just does what it's supposed to while my mind floats somewhere else.

Right now, it's floating back in time. To the weekend.

It was nothing really special. But I did get to hang out with Bri on Saturday. Her dad had to run errands, so he dropped her off for the afternoon. We played board games and watched YouTube videos, mostly. We also talked.

Yeah, of course she's right. And I do get tired of being . . . well, me, sometimes. But I **can't stand** when Bri gets righteous and bossy about it. It's easy for her. I know she's a little nerdy, but she's also outgoing and attracts friends. And she's smart, so naturally she has more things to say.

My parents always try to get me to open up, too. Especially my mom, who's pretty chatty. Then again, she talks enough for the both of us.

I'm more easygoing around my parents, but I don't exactly tell them my secrets. There's **no way**. That's just too embarrassing.

↑ flashback

Sometimes I think it's easier to stay quiet. There's no drama. I can be left alone to daydream or draw. But other times, it really bothers me. I guess that's why I get the squeezy stomach.

"the knots"
↓

Bri coughs, and my mind jolts back to the present.

erase
erase

scritch
scribble
scratch

crumple

HA HA
HA

Settle down,
girls.

sorry

giggle

I REALLY DON'T HAVE TIME TO THINK ABOUT WHAT HAPPENED. I'M LATE FOR HEALTH. AS SOON AS I ARRIVE...

Relocating to the library.

Sorry, people, it's just for a little while.

YESSS!!

random "policing" teacher

Keep it quiet in the halls, folks.

WHEN WE GET THERE, MY PEEPS AND I SNAG A COZY TABLE IN THE BACK. PERFECT FOR SNEAK-TEXTING.

texting Tyler

texting each other

clicky clicky clicky clicky

TYLER AND I HAVE OUR FIRST DEEPLY MEANING-FUL CONVERSATION.

him

me → sup?

Nothing. U?

Nothing. Library.

Cool.   :-)

I'VE NEVER FELT THIS WAY BEFORE. AND I SENSE NEITHER HAS HE.

I've never felt like this.

Really? ♥♥

yeah, I think I ate a bad pizza.

I NOTICE THAT QUIET GIRL IN THE CORNER WITH HER BFF...THE SMART ONE...WHAT'S HER NAME? BRITTANY? BEYONCÉ?

Hey, isn't that the girl who wrote Tyler the—

shhh!

:blip:
Still there?

TYLER KEEPS TEXTING, AND I DON'T WANT TO LOSE FOCUS.

Let's not talk about her, okay? Look — Tyler sent me a love emoji!

You mean that pizza and frowny face?

WE CONTINUE ANALYZING TYLER'S ROMANTIC TEXTS UNTIL IT'S TIME TO GO.

EMMIE

Soon enough, Mr. Bauman announces the heat has been fixed. I reluctantly tear myself away from the library table and head back to class.

Sometimes health class is interesting (the class on reproduction was pretty entertaining), and sometimes it's downright dull (food and nutrition . . . ugh. With a mother like mine, I could teach a class on that).

Today we're continuing a discussion on self-esteem. Mr. Bauman is having us create a collage that describes what we are like "as a person" and also our "hopes and dreams" and "positive personality traits."

I've been pretty stuck.

Still, this beats last week, when we spent an hour listening to a lecture on body odor.

After a few minutes of riffling through twenty-year-old magazines, I find some arts-and-crafts stuff and begin cutting out pictures. Then I see some cute animals and cut those out, too. I adore animals. My parents aren't "pet people," so we've never had any—unless you count dead goldfish and houseplants. (True story: I once tied a string around my mom's minicactus, pretended it was a puppy, and dragged it around the house. Note: prickers in the rug **hurt**.)

Fido

Mr. Bauman comes around to check on our collages. He sees mine and kinda scrutinizes it for a minute. Talk about being under a microscope.

Actually, those gaps kind of **do** describe my personality.

That's it, I need a break. I head across the room to look for more magazines.

As I walk past the other desks, I feel like people are watching me. No one ever, **ever** looks at me. This is kind of unsettling. I wish I had a pile of books to bury my head in. Then again, one of these days it might stick there.

permanent bookface

I start to hear this low, weird snickering behind me. Not really sure, but I think it's Joe Lungo. He's always goofing around.

snorfle snicker

If you're wondering about Joe Lungo, I didn't know him until I got to middle school. He had gone to an elementary school across town—the one that's actually **on** a lakefront.

Dry Valley Elementary

Joe Lungo, acting like an idiot (I imagine)

Because our middle school is so big, they divide each grade into three "teams" with their own teachers. Joe Lungo was on my sixth-grade team, the Periodic Tabletops. And with my usual luck, he also landed on my seventh-grade team.

ptooey

Hock tooey

The Petri Dishes

The Petri Dishes

The Petri Dishes

The Petri Dishes

He's pretty obnoxious. The boys like him because he's a jokester. The girls can't stand him. It's hard to tell if he's going to be one of those people who outgrows his obnoxiousness or carries it with him to adulthood.

Joe L. now

50% chance of future obnoxiousness

BELCHHH

sits around and trolls blogs

TOOT

BODY SNATCHER

50% chance of shedding obnoxiousness

Well, hello. Pleased to make your acquaintance.

gainfully employed

No one is safe from Joe L. I try to stay out of his way, but it's hard when he sits near me in class. He zeroes in on people's weaknesses, and I have plenty.

HA HA HA
"Katie!"

Anyway, back to the snickering . . .

Holy horror, I know that poem. It can't be. It . . .
NONONONO.

I race to the girls' bathroom.

I hide in another stall and cry for, like, ten minutes. I can't believe this is happening. The note. How did he get the note?

Not only am I fresh joke bait for Joe Lungo, but he's **friends** with Tyler Ross. That means he probably already showed the note to him. The only thing I can do is beg Joe L. to give it back.

But what good would that do? It's already out there.

I am the laughingstock of Lakefront. I am finished! I am toast! I am flaming, scorched, dropped-on-the-floor toast!

Someone knocks on my stall door.

BACK IN HEALTH. WE'RE DOING COLLAGES ON SELF-ESTEEM. I ADMIT, IT'S HARD FITTING ALL MY LIKES, HOPES, AND DREAMS ON ONE LITTLE 14×17 SHEET OF PAPER.

LUCKILY, I MANAGE TO FINISH AHEAD OF SCHEDULE. THIS GIVES ME TIME TO DWELL ON THE LATEST HALL HAPPENINGS.

Uh... wow.

me, musing

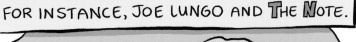

FOR INSTANCE, JOE LUNGO AND THE NOTE.

It's for Tyler Ross.

What?

SQUEAAAL!

AT FIRST, I WONDER IF PEOPLE WILL THINK HE WROTE IT HIMSELF AS A PRACTICAL JOKE.

BUT NO, SCRATCH THAT. THE NOTE IS GOOD... MUSHY BUT WELL STRUCTURED (I HAVE AN A IN ENGLISH). PLUS JOE'S HORRIBLE AT WRITING.

ANYWAY, EMMA (?) NEVER DID ANYTHING TO HIM. POOR THING BARELY EXISTS TO HIM.

SO YEAH, THEY'LL KNOW SHE WROTE IT.

I'LL SAY ONE THING ABOUT THE QUIET GIRL. SHE HAS GREAT TASTE.

I FEEL A WEIRD NEED TO HELP THIS GIRL. MAYBE BECAUSE SHE'S SUCH A QUIET THING. I FEEL KINDA SORRY FOR HER.

SHE'S PRETTY UPSET. I'D BE TOO. BUT I'D ALSO PLOT SOME KIND OF PAYBACK.

sniffle

Maybe we can TP his house. Or put toothpaste in his Oreos or something.

WHEN WE GET BACK, MR. BAUMAN IS WRAPPING UP HIS POST PROJECT SPEECH. THAT MEANS THE BOYS ARE KEEPING THEIR TRAPS SHUT.

scritch scritch

snicker

LOOKS LIKE I HAVE A NEW MISSION NOW.

growlll

deadlier withering glare

ulp

EMMIE

I'm dying. Dead. Done. My life is **over**.

But first I have to go to Spanish.

The good news: it's right next door to health class, and none of those boys—including Tyler Ross—are in it.

The bad news: I've been humiliated into a puddle of slime (see Prologue).

Can this situation get any worse?

The next forty minutes go by in a slow haze. I hand in my quiz to Señora Quell. I have no idea what's on it.

Now I have to walk all the way across the building to history class. I take my ten deep breaths and race out the door before anyone else. I probably run faster than I did during Sprint Day in gym.

I can't believe Joe Lungo bared my soul to Tyler Ross. There's no way I can face anyone at school—especially you-know-who.

Just when my nightmare can't get any worse . . .

BY NOW, YOU'RE PROBABLY WONDERING WHY I'M NOT JEALOUS OF EMMIE. I MEAN, SHE <u>DID</u> WRITE MY BF A LOVE POEM.

TRUTH IS, SHE'S NICE AND ALL. BUT SHE'S NOT EXACTLY... THREATENING.

EMMIE

I **really** take my time getting to class. I take a different route than usual. To my extreme relief, most of the kids in this wing are sixth graders who wouldn't know me from their armpit.

I check my phone. A little past one o'clock. Three classes to get through until I can go home: history, math, and art. I have a feeling this is gonna be the longest two and a half hours of my life. Not that it matters if I'm dead, anyway.

My fantasy funeral

ME →
(literally died of humiliation)

Tyler Ross
(with my
tear-stained
note)

the whole school
gathered in regret

I sliwwer ("slink" plus "cower") up the stairs to history.

When I'm not trying to find a hole to crawl into, I think about what just happened with Tyler Ross.

He didn't pretend like I wasn't there and sliwwer past me, like this:

He didn't smirk or crack a joke at my expense to cover up his own embarrassment, like this:

No. He said . . . "hi."

But why? Does he feel bad about what happened? Does he feel sorry for me? Or does he . . . maybe . . . like the note?

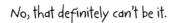

mushy-gushy, with words like "evermore" and "freckle"

No, that definitely can't be it.

124

EMMIE

I take a last-minute detour and stop at my locker. I just have to check.

shuffle
shuffle
shove

Yep, it's really gone.

no
note

It must've fallen out of my English binder after lunch. I'm so stupid! I should've held on to it with both hands.

How am I going to face everybody in my next class? If I'm lucky, only a couple of people know.

I walk (with my last half ounce of hope) to history.

Well, that answers that. Joe Lungo must've spread the word faster than wildfire.

A comparison chart				
random act of nature	spreads fast	affects lives	burns badly	can be put out
wildfire	✓	✓	✓	✓
Joe's mouth	✓	✓	✓	✗

Don't cry, I tell myself. Easier said than done. It takes every fiber in my body to keep the tears at bay. Plus, my desk is in the middle row (if you think the front is worse in this situation, guess again).

snickering kids in front of me

middle of snicker sandwich

snickering kids behind me

Q: Is it possible to disappear into a stack of books?

At least Mr. Musko starts up right away and I can take refuge in his monotone. If those kids didn't stop snickering before, they will now.

I think the only thing that'll make me feel better is to find Brianna. I really need to talk to her.

As if she read my mind again, my phone starts vibrating, and the tiny little window lights up with her number.

I hide behind my giant history textbook, flip open my phone, and scroll to Bri's text.

She sounds panicked. And upset.

Meet after
class.
Usual spot.
Panicked!!
And upset!!

Uh-oh. Now what?

I put up with Mr. Musko's death drone for forty minutes, then the bell rings. Then I rip out of there faster than, well . . .

HISTORY ENDS AND I WALK OUT WITH MY BFFs. SUDDENLY, I LOSE INTEREST IN THE TALK ABOUT YOUTUBE MAKEUP TUTORIALS. I THINK I'LL WAIT FOR TYLER. AFTER ALL, HE'S MY BF NOW.

THIS CAN'T BE HAPPENING.
IT'S <u>EMMIE</u>. SHE'S SWEET AND
ALL, BUT SHE'S NO THREAT.

shinier hair

more confident

friendlier

more athletic

RIGHT?

EMMIE

Brianna and I have a favorite meeting spot. It's almost a hide-away. On the second floor's main hallway, there's this halfway point. It's like a stairwell to nowhere. At one time it did go some-where. There was a lot of speculation around it.

secret attic?

point of origin for dead rat?

Narnia?

Student of the month

FIRE

Anyway, it's blocked off now. There's a gate at the landing, and a couple of steps beneath it. It's also tucked into a side corner, so most kids forget it's there.

Brianna and I have a habit of meeting in this spot whenever there's a crisis. Usually, it's me needing last-minute math help or her needing a last-minute snack (I started carrying yogurt-covered peanuts in my bag). Or sometimes it's just to talk.

me and Bri, sharing hopes and dreams and favorite YouTubers between classes

But today is different. It's an actual emergency. Which is why I need my best friend.

How did this happen, Em?

Huh?

Just as I feared . . . Joe Lungo didn't just show it to my classmates. . . . He texted it to everyone! Well, except to me . . . since I have that dumb phone that doesn't receive photos.

I start crying. Hard.

Bri sits with me until I calm down a little, but I can tell she's really upset too.

I explain what I know. How the note disappeared. How Joe L. somehow found it and recited it in health class.

OMG, I forgot I had Bri's note. I had picked up both of them.

139

EMMIE

I have to get back to my locker and make sure Brianna's note is still there, even if that means I'm late. I race to the first floor. My hands are shaking so much, I mess up the combination twice. I finally get it right and fling open the door.

For the second time I riffle quickly through my binder and . . . **whew!**

Bri's note

I let out a long sigh of relief. Finally, something has gone right today. For a split second I'm almost glad I dropped my note and not hers. But then I remember how Bri said she wouldn't forgive me if I lost her note, and suddenly, I'm both mad and sad at once. Would she really have ditched me as a friend?

I shoot Bri a quick, curt text to let her know her note is safe. Then I snap the phone shut and turn it off. I don't feel like hearing back from her.

I still have two minutes to get to class. All I want to do is just stand here. Or go home. But I don't. Some weird alien force picks me up and guides me to class.

Math.

I hate math.

Tyler Ross is in my class, but he sits toward the back. I sit in the second row, so I can't stare at him. Maybe that's good. I'm already bad at math, and staring would probably make any small thing I **do** learn blow right out of my brain.

Anyway, it doesn't matter because at this point, I really, really, **really** don't want to be anywhere near him.

As if that isn't bad enough, Joe Lungo is also in my class. He sits right in front of Tyler Ross.

I'm the last one to class, but luckily, I make it just before the bell rings. Once I sit down, I hear that oh-so-familiar snickering.

Humiliation complete.

EMMIE

I hide in the girls' restroom until my last class starts. **Just have to make it through one more period**, I tell myself. Can't help but notice I've been talking to myself a **lot** today. And hiding in the bathroom.

This is getting
<u>so</u> unoriginal

Not sure how I manage to get the whole place to myself. Maybe Baked Bean Girl finally exploded. Maybe the makeup crowd decided it was too late in the day to impress anyone. I'm just grateful nobody knows I'm here.

what's left of
baked bean girl

I cry to get it all out of my system. I have a surprisingly quick
cry, which is good timing since my next class begins soon. I think
it's quick because on top of being totally humiliated, I'm mad.
Angry crying is faster than sad crying. Also more violent.

knife
tears

I'm mad at Tyler Ross and his friends.
I'm mad at Brianna.

Most of all, I'm mad at myself.

How could I let this happen? My mom says things usually happen for a reason. I'm still trying to sort that one out. Maybe my emotional wreckage was meant to amuse everyone? If so, mission totally accomplished.

I splash water on my face. My eyes are kind of bloodshot, but I don't really care anymore. I've decided that tomorrow I'm going to play sick, and then I'm going to move to Singapore. (Or any other foreign city. I just like the way Singapore sounds.)

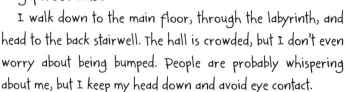

I walk down to the main floor, through the labyrinth, and head to the back stairwell. The hall is crowded, but I don't even worry about being bumped. People are probably whispering about me, but I keep my head down and avoid eye contact.

dead rat
(may have moved
an inch)

spleen very "agitated"
and "unflowery"

Art is my last class. It's in the basement. I'm guessing it's down there because of all the fumes.

Degas

O'Keefe

STAY AWAY FROM DRUGS

PLOP

clay

Normally, it's my favorite class, but now all I care about is making it to the final bell. Today I'm especially glad it's in the basement because it's away from civilization (a.k.a. away from humiliation). More good news: art is an elective, so Joe Lungo and most of my other classmates aren't in it.

The bad news: Tyler Ross is.

He started taking art this year. I've wondered why. He's usually into sports. My guess is all the other electives were taken, and art is a time filler.

I make a promise to myself not to look at him all period and focus on my project. Just one more class to get through.

But then, as soon as I reach the top of the stairs, there they are: the fearsome threesome. Tyler Ross, Anthony Randall, and Joe Lungo. I stop dead.

the only working water fountain

ptooey

They see me.
I'm trapped.

I have to walk past them.

I imagine I'm the color of beets. (I hate beets.) I work up all my nerve to ignore them and step by, but then Joe gets this huge, evil grin on his face and opens his mouth.

I start to get really warm, like there's a fire kindling in my face. But it's not embarrassment—it's something else. Then the unexpected happens.

And then something **really** unexpected happens.

For a while Tyler Ro— **Tyler** and I can't stop laughing. It's like all this pent-up stuff inside finally burst out.

I guess Tyler was fed up with Joe Lungo too.

After a minute or so we start to calm down. I don't know what to say, but I'm still laughing a little. It feels good. Tyler asks me if I'm heading down to art. I say yes.

To my extreme relief, he doesn't talk about the note. My heart's nearly pounding out of my chest, though. It pounds so hard, I feel like it's gonna make Tyler's freckle jump off his face.

He asks if I finished our assignment. We've been working on

it for so long, it's taken up our whole quarter. Hesitantly, I pull out my drawing and show it to him.

I'm so surprised. I didn't know Tyler was such a good artist.

I decide then and there that I'm gonna try to put my humiliation away for a while. I'm just so tired of feeling bad about everything that happened.

Maybe it's working because suddenly, I kind of forget that I was embarrassed.

In fact, I forget a bunch of things.

ART CLASS

EMMIE

In art class all the desks are pushed together to form a big square. That way, if we're doing a still life or something, it can be set up in the middle of the square and we can paint it from all angles.

fake flowers

fake crystal vase

X-ACTO scratch

real book

booger

glue gun stain

paint stain

Today we're just working on our zentangles. They're due right before winter break. Ms. Laurie is going around the room, checking on everyone's progress.

Tyler is talking to me. I can't believe it!

I'm sort of forgetting about the incident. Tyler makes it easier by joking around. And I'm kind of joking back.

For some reason, I find that my heart is not beating as fast anymore. It's weird talking to him, but it also feels kind of natural—like hanging out with Brianna.

Wow. I was so busy talking, I forgot to be nervous.

I'm disappointed he has to go back to his seat 'cause it's on the other side of the square. But then the girl next to me says something.

quiet girl who's also in my history class

I feel better. Sarah and I keep talking, this time about our (horrible!) history homework, an upcoming test, how unfair it is that we can't use oil paints yet, and the school's art show. We both want to make it in. Sarah predicts that she probably won't and I definitely will.

With surprise, I realize I haven't just talked to one new person but two. **Me**. Two people. And one was a boy, and I didn't melt into a pool of goo or burst into flames or anything. To think, this morning I could barely mutter "excuse me" to those boys by my locker.

Maybe it's not as hard as I thought.

SOMETHING'S HAPPENING TO ME. I TRY TO SPEAK, BUT I CAN'T.

I WALK DOWN THE HALL, BUT NO ONE SAYS HI OR JOINS ME.

TYLER ACTS LIKE I DON'T EXIST NOW.

EMMIE

The unthinkable.

The bell rings, and I'm walking out with two new friends. At least I think they're new friends. I hope so.

I go over the day in my head. I feel better, not so crushed. My stomach hasn't had the knots since last period. I'm even walking taller. My spine must be breathing.

uh-oh.

Boys.
But . . . so what?
They're just . . . boys.

Wow. I think I'm actually okay.

I start to walk out. But all of a sudden, I remember some-thing. And I get a little lonely.

We head onto Brianna's bus to find seats.

EMMIE

I tell Brianna the whole truth. How I've always wanted to be:

Sometimes she had the kind of life I wish I had.

And sometimes she just helped me deal with stuff.

In my head, when I couldn't say something, she said it for me.

Why?

Your friends are immature, and you don't stand up to them. I don't like cowards.

When I couldn't defend myself, she did it for me.

And when I was upset, she made me feel better.

But for the first time...

The bus engine starts up, and I feel my seat vibrate. I look over at Brianna. I worry that she thinks I'm nuts.

Suddenly, I'm grateful for my brainiac friend. I realize she's not just book smart but also feelings smart. I look back out the window so she doesn't see me get all misty again.

Yeah, it did start out that way.

But then, who would've thought things would turn around...

Or that I'd be the one to do it?

Me, for a change . . .
And no one else.

EPILOGUE (And you thought it was over!)

So that's the story of how I changed from a human being into a puddle of slime, and back into a human being again.

It didn't end there, actually. I went to Brianna's, and then my mom picked me up on her way home from work. I even managed to get my math homework done with Bri's help.

I also gave her note back. She stashed it in a safe spot.

Bri's note: in the bottom of a box in the bottom of a bottom drawer in the back of her closet

So now here I sit in the car with my mom. She's telling me about her day.

Then she asks me about mine.
I pause. Should I tell her what happened?
At first, I think:

Then I think:

Besides, I don't have to tell her **everything**.

I take a deep breath.

I made some new friends. You'll never guess how...

ACKNOWLEDGMENTS

I'd like to thank everyone who helped bring **Invisible Emmie** to life:

Michael, my wonderful husband and biggest supporter. He always believes in me even when I don't.

My daughters, Mollie and Nikki, who inspire me just by being their funny, authentic, vibrant selves.

My mom, dad, brother, and sister, who encouraged me to draw. I don't think they realized what a monster they created.

Aaron, my other great cheerleader.

My agent, Dan Lazar, who is a dynamic, dedicated, hardworking machine.

My editor, Donna Bray, who really knows her stuff and can read minds. Somehow she seems to connect with whatever I'm thinking.

My art director, Katie Fitch, who was able to get married and still have time to do the monstrous job of laying out this amazing-looking book.

Everyone at Harper Collins USA and Writer's House for their nonstop support and expertise.

Mina, Kyla, and Gabi, who read and reviewed the first draft of the book. You guys rock.

Stephan, who is to blame for originally encouraging me to do this. Your fault. And thank you.

The rest of my family and friends, whom I've probably bored to tears discussing the evolution of Emmie. Endless thanks for your patience and support.